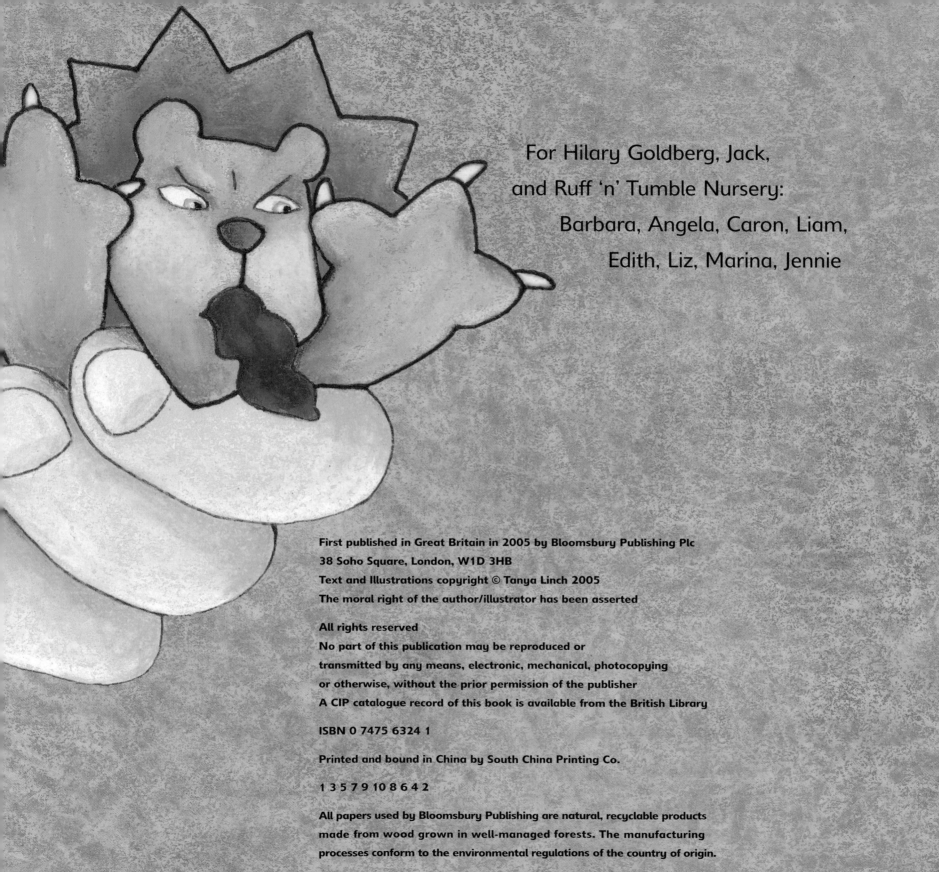

For Hilary Goldberg, Jack,
and Ruff 'n' Tumble Nursery:
Barbara, Angela, Caron, Liam,
Edith, Liz, Marina, Jennie

First published in Great Britain in 2005 by Bloomsbury Publishing Plc
38 Soho Square, London, W1D 3HB
Text and Illustrations copyright © Tanya Linch 2005
The moral right of the author/illustrator has been asserted

ISBN 0 7475 6324 1

Printed and bound in China by South China Printing Co.

1 3 5 7 9 10 8 6 4 2

All papers used by Bloomsbury Publishing are natural, recyclable products
made from wood grown in well-managed forests. The manufacturing
processes conform to the environmental regulations of the country of origin.

The Owl, the Aat, and the Roar

Tanya Linch

BLOOMSBURY
CHILDREN'S
BOOKS

The Owl and the Aat used to ride in the front pouch of Ben's bag on their way to nursery. They loved it there because that's where Ben's mum put his biscuits for later!

Sometimes Mum forgot to zip up the pouch and they'd hang over the edge to nibble the biscuits and watch the outside.

Nearly every day they would see a cat
or a dog, or stop at the wall to say hello
to the birdie that lived on the other side.

Ben picked up sticks and stones that his mum put in the pouch, so there was always something for the Owl and the Aat to play with at nursery if things got quiet for them.

At home time, Mum would take out the biscuits and give them to Ben. He and Mum never noticed that the Owl and the Aat had been nibbling them.

They just supposed the crumbly bits round the edges were from being squashed in the bag all afternoon.

Then, on the way home,
the Owl and
the Aat liked to bump up and down in the bag as they all went down the hill.

Everyone was happy, until ...

One day Ben decided to take the Roar to nursery, too. The Roar was a different sort of character altogether.

He was loud and noisy and angry.

He liked to bite the Aat on the nose and make him cry.

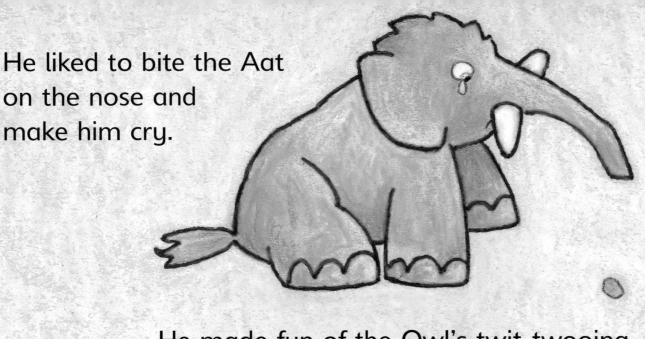

He made fun of the Owl's twit-twooing, saying it wasn't nearly as good as his loud roar!

And he thought it was funny to smash up the biscuits with his tail.

Soon Mum began to notice that something was going on. At home time she would wonder why the biscuits were crushed. Ben would kick and scream because he didn't want crumbs!

Mum had a terrible time trying to push them in the buggy. The Owl, the Aat, and the Roar were fighting in the bag and Ben was twisting and turning about.

The next day Ben put the Roar in the front pouch again! And at nursery he took him out to play. The Roar was so proud to be chosen to meet Ben's friends.

'Ha ha!' thought the Roar. 'I bet the Owl and the Aat aren't having nearly as much fun as I am.

I'm the best!'

At home time, Mum appeared, scooped Ben up, kissed him, and off they went.

'**Hey!**' shouted the Roar.

'**What about me?**'

But before the Roar could do anything about it, he was cleared up
with all the other nursery animals, put in a large tin box,
and left on the high shelf with the rest of the toys.

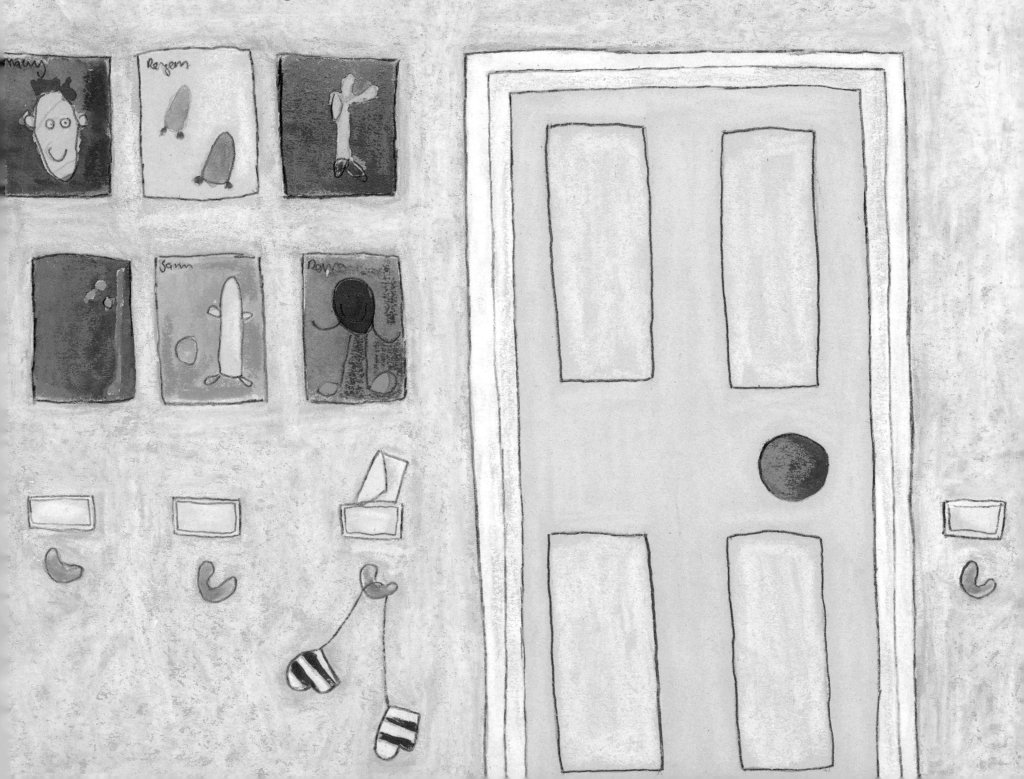

The nursery went very quiet when
the last of the children had left, and then
the lights went off, and moonlight
came in through the window.

The Roar was feeling very scared and alone. He glanced over to see what the other animals were doing, but they weren't nearly as friendly as the Owl and the Aat.

There was a **huge**
crocodile with sharp teeth,

and a lion that was
much bigger
than the Roar,

and a l o n g, l o n g snake

with a slithery long tongue.

The Roar was so scared that he stayed still all night, and tears rolled down his little face.

The next day the lights went on. All the
animals were tipped on to the table,
and the Roar landed with a bump.

Ben ran in, picked up the
Roar straightaway and
gave him to Mum to
put in the bag with
the Owl and
the Aat.

The Roar was so pleased to be back in the bag
with the Owl and the Aat, that
he didn't pick on them at all.

The Owl and the Aat couldn't stay cross with
the Roar for long. At home time, not two
but three of them hung out of the pouch.

Ben smiled as he ate his biscuits, which weren't in crumbs any more. They had just been nibbled at the corners ...

By the same author

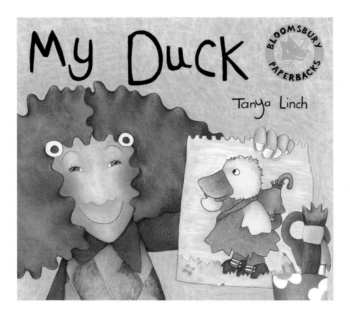

My Duck
Tanya Linch

'Tanya Linch's *My Duck* is a cautionary tale for those about to begin full-time education, and for those about to teach them.'
The Scotsman